THE SNACK BAR
SNACK BAR
TO GROCERY STORE
THE LAKE
THE BEST LEMON TREES
THE FORT

For the bike riders in my neighborhood:

Sallie, Beverly, Wendy, Kate, and Brooke.—C. H.

For Teddy and Oskar.—Z. O.

Library of Congress Cataloging-in-Publication Data:

Names: Higgins, Carter, author. | OHora, Zachariah, illustrator.
Title: Bikes for sale / written by Carter Higgins ; illustrated by Zachariah OHora.
Description: San Francisco, California : Chronicle Books LLC, [2019] | Summary: Maurice rides his bike all over selling lemonade, while Lotta rides her bike collecting sticks as she goes; they ride different routes and are completely unaware of each other—until their bikes are wrecked and they meet at Sid's who has turned their damaged bikes into one tandem bike, and a friendship is born.
Identifiers: LCCN 2017061551 | ISBN 9781452159324 (alk. paper)
Subjects: LCSH: Bicycles—Juvenile fiction. | Tandem bicycles—Juvenile fiction. | Friendship—Juvenile fiction. | CYAC: Bicycles and bicycling—Fiction. | Friendship—Fiction. | LCGFT: Picture books.
Classification: LCC PZ7.1.H545 Bi 2019 | DDC 813.6 [E]—dc23 LC record available at https://lccn.loc.gov/2017061551

Manufactured in China.

Design by Jennifer Tolo Pierce.
Typeset in Gibson and Have a Nice Day.
The illustrations in this book were rendered in acrylic on paper.

10 9 8 7 6 5 4 3

Chronicle Books LLC
680 Second Street
San Francisco, California 94107

Chronicle Books—we see things differently. Become part of our community at www.chroniclekids.com.

WRITTEN BY **Carter Higgins**

ILLUSTRATED BY **Zachariah OHora**

chronicle books · san francisco

They were new once.

And then, they weren't.

This one belonged to Maurice.

He rode it to the grocery store,

through the park on 3rd Street that had the best lemon trees, and to the shop.

No matter where he rode, he always had customers.

He was far enough from the grocery store
and just beyond the snack bar in the park.

"Everyone loves lemonade," he thought.

Twenty-five cents wasn't all that much for some squeezy drops of sunshine.

Besides, they'd get to keep the cup.

After a while, it was time to ride on.

"STAY HERE!" said the construction site man, thirsty from all that hammering.

"DON'T GO!" said the dog walker with lots and lots of leashes.

But Maurice had more corners to try.

That one belonged to Lotta.

She rode it to the woods,

through the ditch on 5th Street that had the best mud, and to the fort.

No matter where she rode, she always had room for one more.

She rode deep into the woods where the sun couldn't reach,
and far out to the lake where the beavers
kept their leftovers.

"Everyone loves sticks," she thought.
"They're the best thing to collect."

Besides, they were free.

After a while, it was time to ride on.

"DON'T GO!" said the dog walker with lots and lots of leashes.

"STAY HERE!" said the bunch of boys who couldn't pick a favorite.

But Lotta had more thickets to try.

He rode

and she rode

and they rode all over.

But what looked like a small stick was really a smashup,

and that was the end of this one.

Maurice walked home instead.

And what looked like some petals was really some peels,

and that was the end of that one.

Lotta walked too.

They were new once.

And then, they weren't.

Maurice found some okay sneakers.

Lotta got galoshes.

They tried to forget where their wheels had gone.

But sneakers weren't as fast as rubber tires. And galoshes weren't good for climbing.

So the people were thirsty for sunshine.

And the sticks stayed stuck on their trees.

MEANWHILE . . .

To someone new, the rust sparkled.

The deflated tires still held hope.

Sid knew all about the bikes.

The satchel told stories of sugar.

The bell ding-a-linged of a ditch.

The sprockets remembered mud and lemons, twigs and mint.

On this side, Maurice wondered.

On that side, Lotta maybe'd.

And then they went to see Sid.

SALE

Lotta rode her bike to the woods,

through the park on 3rd Street that had the best lemon trees,

and through the ditch on 5th Street that had the best mud.

Maurice rode his bike to the grocery store,

through the park on 3rd Street that had the best lemon trees,

to the woods, and to the shop.

They'd never ridden this way before.

CHOMPER

They had new adventures.

Now the lemons had more shine

and the sticks had more snap.

What looked like a friend was really a friend,
and that's how friendships begin.

They are new once.

And then, they aren't.

← SHORTCUT TO SID'S BIKE SHOP
THE DITCH
(WITH THE BEST MUD)
THE PARK